If found, please return to

<u>Rufus</u> _____ the Menace.

You can find me hiding in

4 Hanworth rd, TW12 3DH
Hampton   Middlesex

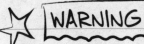

You look a bit like

☆ | **WARNING** | *If this should end up in the enemy hands*

of a Softy (you boring bonces know who you are) it **WILL**

self-destruct **IMMEDIATELY!**

WATCH OUT!

MEGA PANTS

When you've finished this journal,
write the word 'PANTS' twenty times
throughout the pages, then challenge a
Menacing Mate to find them all.

PUFFIN BOOKS

UK | USA | Canada | Ireland | Australia
India | New Zealand | South Africa

Puffin Books is part of the Penguin Random House group of companies
whose addresses can be found at global.penguinrandomhouse.com.

puffinbooks.com

First published 2015
001

Written by Lauren Holowaty
Illustrations by Steve May

The moral right of the author and illustrator has been asserted

Printed in Great Britain by Clays Ltd, St Ives plc

A CIP catalogue record for this book is available from the British Library

ISBN: 978–0–141–35795–9

www.greenpenguin.co.uk

MENACE IT Yourself!

SCRIBBLE JOURNAL

Illustrated by Steve May

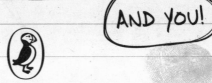

AND YOU!

PUFFIN

Real Menaces are **SUPER** good at doodling all over things!

Do you like the cover of this book? What would you do better? Design a new cover on the next page, then tear it out and slap it on top of the real one!

TIP: Remember to put your name on it, so everyone knows what a mega-brilliant doodling **MENACE** you are.

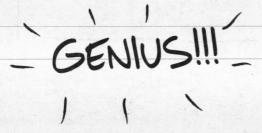

GENIUS!!!

Design your cover here! ⟶ ⟱

Write your name in the space here! ⟶

❋ the Diary of ❋

❋ THE MENACE ❋

MY BEDROOM

is where I come up with all my

genius menacing ideas!

What would you scrawl all over your room if

you could? Draw and decorate your room

Menace-style here! ⟶

3

STRICTLY (NO) SOFTIES, TEACHERS OR GROWN-UPS!

(THAT INCLUDES YOU, MUM AND DAD!)

It's super important for an International Menace of Mystery like me to have privacy. This is the sign I stick on my bedroom door to keep out unwanted intruders. Design your own sign on the next page, then **WHACK** it on your door.

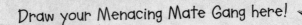
Draw your Menacing Mate Gang here!

YOUR MENACING MATE GANG!

Draw the Menaces you respect here!

MENACES YOU RESPECT

MY KNOW-IT-ALL
BUM-FACED ENEMIES

Super-Softy
Walter

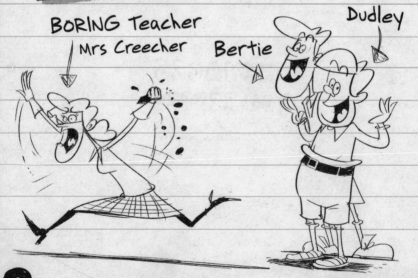

BORING Teacher
Mrs Creecher

Bertie

Dudley

MAKE A LIST OF WAYS
TO IDENTIFY
BUM-FACED ENEMIES

- LOVE doing homework

- Always being sneaky

- Stuck-up

- Name is Alexia Enright

-

-

-

TOP-SECRET BASE

Every good Menace has to have one of these, and tree houses are the best bases to hang out and stash stuff in! Plus, you can snoop on others, but they can't snoop on you. **HA!**

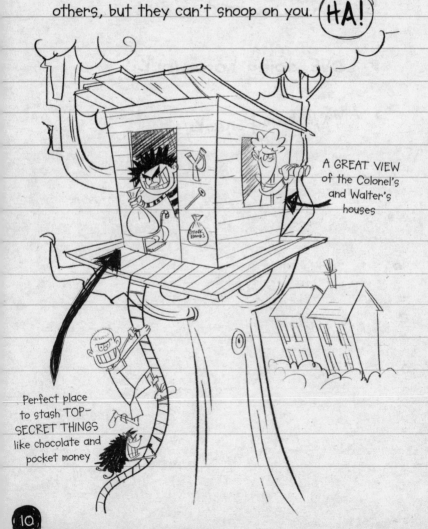

A GREAT VIEW of the Colonel's and Walter's houses

Perfect place to stash TOP-SECRET THINGS like chocolate and pocket money

What goes in your tree house? Remember to include lots of **menacing equipment**, inventions, chocolate and **anti-Softy defence mechanisms!**

SoFTY-PROOF CODE

Make up your own Secret Softy-proof Code so those smarty-pants swotties will be super stumped! **Draw a different symbol** under each letter to create a code that only you (and your Menacing Mates!) will understand.

A	B	C	D	E	F
G	H	I	J	K	L
M	N	O	P	Q	R
S	T	U	V	W	X
Y	Z	!	?		

Take that, archest-enemies!

NOW USE YOUR SECRET SOFTY-PROOF
CODE to write a message that only your fellow
Menaces will understand. **BWA-HA-HA!!!**

THINGS I LIKE . . .

STUPIDO!

THINGS I HATE...

ARE YOU A MENACE OR A SOFTY?

So you think you're really a Menace? Use this chart to double-check.

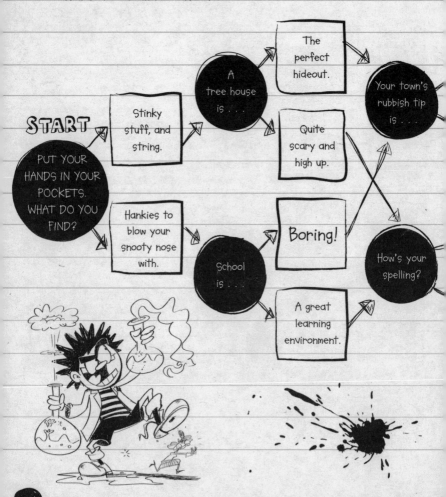

START

PUT YOUR HANDS IN YOUR POCKETS. WHAT DO YOU FIND?

Stinky stuff, and string.

Hankies to blow your snooty nose with.

A tree house is . . .

The perfect hideout.

Quite scary and high up.

School is . . .

Boring!

A great learning environment.

Your town's rubbish tip is . . .

How's your spelling?

16.

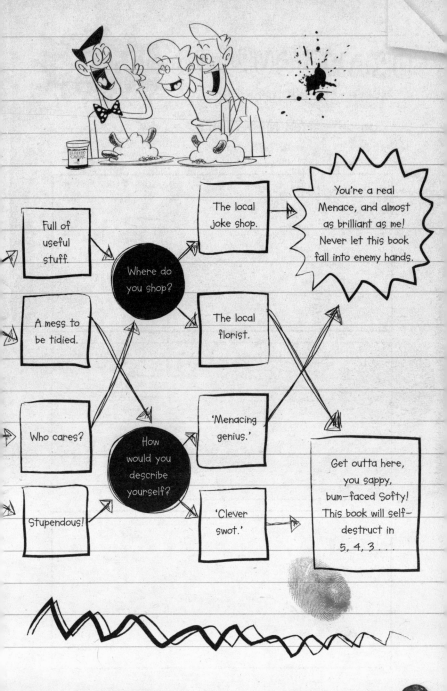

DRAW YOUR OWN COMIC

where you get turned into

an ant-sized Mini-Menace . . .

TIP: Why not use some of these?

HELLO!

WATCH OUT!

SPLAT!

THINK!

19.

 **BEANOTOWN BURGERS** → THE BEST RESTAURANT IN THE WHOLE UNIVERSE!

This is my usual:

the Slopper-Gnosher-Gut-Bustin' Burger

with extra tomato sauce, of course!

Draw your dream mega-burger here, and give it a mega-munching name.

 CHOMP!

My mate
Pie Face
LOVES pies!

What are the
yummiest-ever
pie fillings you can
think of? **Write
them down here.**

What would you
put in a **prank** pie
to give to a Softy?
Maybe you'd put a
spring underneath
it to **SPLAT** them
in the face!

A true Menace like me has to think on their feet. Fill in these **FUNNY NOTES** to put on people's backs as fast as you can!

I smell!!

I love soppy kittens

I have one brain cell and here it is

Kick me Quick

FANTASTIC!

23

The one thing I look forward to at **boring** old school is **BREAK TIME!** The first person to reach the top of the climbing frame is **King for the Rest of the Day**, and it's **ALWAYS** me!!! Design your own brilliant climbing frame here.

This is my design!

<u>A true Menace</u> should never leave the house without their BMS (Basic Menacing Supplies). You never know when you might come

FACE-TO-BUM-FACE

with a flower-loving Softy!

I'm always carrying super-useful things like my secret mini water blaster, **fake spider,** fake worm, fake creepy-crawly, **fake Gnasher poo,** string and, of course, my **mega slingshot!**

What do you keep in your backpack and
pockets? List it all here. ⤷

Keep an eye on your LOCAL SOFTIES, and record your observations here. These observations will be CRUCIAL for when you want to menace them.

TIP 1:

Note down their **weaknesses, likes** and **dislikes** to maximize your future **menacing potential.**

TIP 2:

Always try to blend into your surroundings and **NEVER** be spotted. Dark masks and hats are useful for this.

MY OBSERVATIONS

PLAYGROUND
BOOBY TRAPS

are **BRILLIANT**! Draw as many as you can think of here.

YOUR MENACING DIARY

It's time to do some menacing every day for a week. Now we're talking!

Use this section to keep a record of what great stuff you did to **menace grown-ups**. It will soon be the **most important book** in the **universe!**

MONDAY

TUESDAY

WEDNESDAY

THURSDAY

FRIDAY

SATURDAY

DROOL

SUNDAY

Think you've spotted a
WET-LETTUCE WHINGER?
Use this list to check.

SOFTY-CHECKER

❶ Do they look like a **bum-face?** YES/NO

❷ Do they have a **smarmy smile?** YES/NO

❸ Do they say **BORING**, uninteresting things that make you want to **snooze? Zzzzzz!** YES/NO

❹ Do they shout '**Spiffo!**' when they get excited? YES/NO

❺ Are they carrying lots of **books** about plants and **stamp collecting?** YES/NO

❻ Do they dress like your **grandad** or like a **grown-up?** YES/NO

Did you answer **YES** to even one the above?

If so, you've probably spotted a **smarmy Softy.**

EEURGH! Best get away, **QUICK!**

This is my all-time

FAVOURITE JUMPER.

What does yours look like?

Design your <u>favourite</u> jumper here.

TARGET PRACTICE

I'm always ready to menace!

Look around your house and write down things that could be used as **catapult ammo** should you need to menace at a minute's notice. Ha!

Use the opposite page for target practice.

REMEMBER! Don't use Mum's favourite vase. Or the cat.

Write your total points in the space below.

TOTAL POINTS:

GUNGE is great for gunging unsuspecting Softies! But what's in it? You decide!

RECIPE FOR GUNGE!

I've included a couple of my own faves to get
you started.

INGREDIENTS

Earwax

_____   _____

Slug Juice

_____   _____

toothpaste
_____   _____

soap
_____   _____

WHAT TO DO WITH YOUR GUNGE

_____

_____

YOUR
PRANK PLANNER

I am the Prankmaster General.

Use the next pages to plan your
pranks and rank them by shading in
the **Menace-o-meter**!

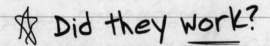

After you've performed your
pranks, ask yourself:

⭐ **Did they work?**

⭐ Did anything go **wrong**?

⭐ **Did you get caught?**

⭐ How could you **improve**
for next time?

PRANK
NAME:_____

PRANK
NUMBER:_____

◉ Who is your target? _____

◉ What equipment will you need?

_____

◉ Who will you tell? ⟶ (Never share your plans with a Softy)

_____

◉ What will you do? _____

◉ How will you make your
   escape afterwards?

   _____

   _____

◉ Menace-o-meter ranking ⟶

10
9
8
7
6
5 MENACE!
4
3
2
1 SNOT!

PRANK NAME: _____   PRANK NUMBER: _____

• Who is your target? _____

• What equipment will you need?

_____

• Who will you tell?

_____

• What will you do? _____

• How will you make your
  escape afterwards?

  _____

  _____

• Menace-o-meter ranking

10
9
8
7
6
5 — MENACE!
4
3
2
1 — SWOT!

PRANK
NAME:_____

PRANK
NUMBER: _____

● Who is your target? _____

● What equipment will you need?

_____

● Who will you tell?

_____

● What will you do? _____

● How will you make your
escape afterwards?

_____

_____

● Menace-o-meter ranking

10
9
8
7
6
5 — MENACE!
4
3
2
1 — SWOT!

51

PRANK NAME: ＿＿＿＿＿＿＿

PRANK NUMBER: ＿＿＿＿＿

- Who is your target? ＿＿＿＿＿＿＿＿＿

- What equipment will you need?

＿＿＿＿＿＿＿＿＿＿＿＿＿＿＿＿

- Who will you tell?

＿＿＿＿＿＿＿＿＿＿＿＿＿＿＿＿

- What will you do? ＿＿＿＿＿＿＿＿＿

- How will you make your escape afterwards?

＿＿＿＿＿＿＿＿＿＿

＿＿＿＿＿＿＿＿＿＿

- Menace-o-meter ranking

10
11
9
8
7
6
5 MENACE!
4
3
2 SNOT!
1

52

PRANK
NAME:_____

PRANK
NUMBER:_____

🔹 Who is your target? _____

🔹 What equipment will you need?

_____

🔹 Who will you tell?

_____

🔹 What will you do? _____

🔹 How will you make your
escape afterwards?

_____

_____

🔹 Menace-o-meter ranking

✦10✦
9
8
7
6
5 — MENACE!
4
3
2
1 — SWOT!

PRANK
NAME: _____

PRANK
NUMBER: _____

⊕ Who is your target? _____

● What equipment will you need?

_____

● Who will you tell?

_____

⊕ What will you do? _____

⊕ How will you make your
escape afterwards?

_____

_____

⊕ Menace-o-meter ranking

```
        * * *
      *  10  *
     *       *
        11 *
        9
        8
        7
        6
    5 -  MENACE!
    4 -
    3 -
    2 -
    1 -  SWOT!
```

PRANK
NAME: _ _ _ _ _ _ _ _ _ _ _

PRANK
NUMBER: _ _ _ _ _ _

* Who is your target? _ _ _ _ _ _ _ _ _ _ _ _ _ _ _ _ _

* What equipment will you need?

_ _

* Who will you tell?

_ _

* What will you do? _ _ _ _ _ _ _ _ _ _ _ _ _ _ _ _ _ _

* How will you make your
escape afterwards?

_ _ _ _ _ _ _ _ _ _ _ _ _ _ _ _

_ _ _ _ _ _ _ _ _ _ _ _ _ _ _ _

* Menace-o-meter ranking

10
11
9
8
7
6
5 MENACE!
4
3
2 SNOT!
1

Put your dirty shoe print on the opposite page to prove that you've been outside menacing!

DRAW YOUR OWN COMIC

where you meet me, Gnasher

and Minnie the Minx . . .

TIP:
Why not use some of these?

SCREECH!

SKID!

SLIDE!

TRICK CAKES

My gran is the <u>coolest</u> gran ever! She is a **Menacing Mastermind** who rides around town on her Charley Davidson motorcycle and makes the **best trick cakes in the world!** Gran's trick cakes are great for luring in Softies, then giving them a gross taste of menacing medicine!

AARGH!

What **GROSS** ingredients would you put in your **trick cakes?**

TIP:
Chilli powder will taste gross and you can sprinkle it on the icing to make Softies sneeze their snooty noses off!

CONSTRUCT A FORT FIT FOR A MENACE!

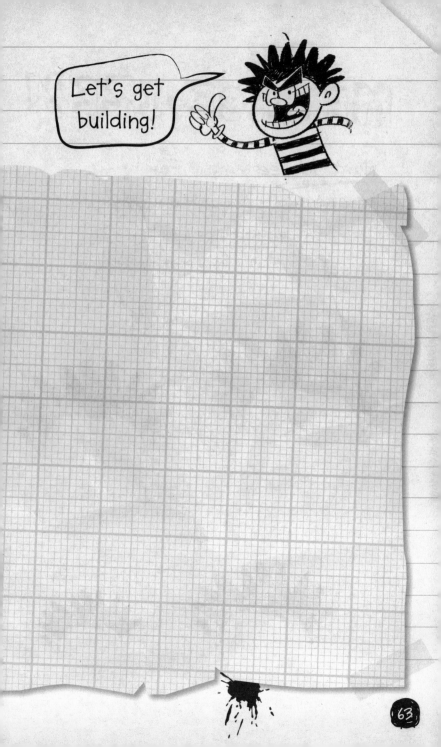

THE
MENACE-IZER!

Want to see how your **family** and **friends** would look as **Menaces?**

Stick photos (or draw pictures) of their faces on this page!

IF YOU SNOOZE, YOU LOSE!

Walter has fallen asleep. You have one **large** black pen. What will you do, my mighty Menacing Mate?

MENACING DOODLE TIPS:

moustache

monobrow

spiky hair

tattoos  *Mummykins*

'Bum-face' on his forehead

(Just a few obvious suggestions!)

Fill this page with as many **funny noises** as you can!
<u>Windy pop</u> noises are especially funny!

Time for some **splashtastic** menacing action! Design your own mega-menacing **water pistol** here!

DRAW YOUR OWN
MENACE!

Here's a **step-by-step guide** to drawing your very own Menace. Follow the instructions and **draw your Menace at the end**.

1 Using a pencil, draw a **big round circle**.

Remember to leave plenty of room for your Menace's body and hair!

2 Draw one **squished**-up little circle **in the middle**, and two bigger ones just above it. Add a couple of dots, and you have your Menace's **eyes** and **nose**.

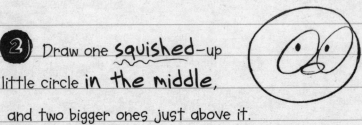

3 Add the **eyebrows**, mouth, hair and one ear. Lots of jagged lines will make your Menace

extra-Menacey!

4 Draw your **Menace's body**. Start with a **stick figure**, then draw the **rough body shape** round it, just like in this picture.

5 Now it's time to **add some detail!**

Use your pencil to add in **fingers**, **socks**, **cuffs** and all the other little touches that make your **Menace a Menace!**

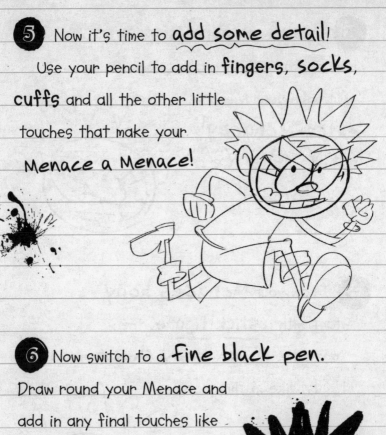

6 Now switch to a **fine black pen.**

Draw round your Menace and add in any final touches like **stripes** and **shoelaces**.

Finally, rub out your **pencil marks** - and you're done!

TOP WORK!

JOIN THE
MENACE SQUAD!

You and your **Menacing Mates** are taking over your town.

Design a team uniform to show you mean **mega-menacing business!**

PRANKING PETS!

My best friend and the greatest pranking partner with paws **EVER** is Gnasher!

GNNNASH!

Gran also has two great four-legged Menacing Mates: **Gnipper** and **Rasher**.

They all help us with our menacing!

What qualities do you look for in a **furry friend**? Draw a picture of your ideal **mini-menacing pal** here. Unless it's a **gorilla**. Then it won't be so mini . . .

SUGARY TREATS
ARE THE BEST!

Especially ice cream!

A **giant tub** of Double Fatties' double—

fat ice cream (butter—banana—chocco—scotch

flavour) is just what I need after a day of

menacing. What's your favourite ice cream?

Draw a giant tub of it here, and stick

loads of extra **treats** on top!

You're going camping.
DOUBLE WHOOP!

What do you take to menace other campers?
Write a list, then **pitch** your tent
by drawing it on the opposite page.

LIST

- Camouflage whoopee cushion

Don't forget your super-duper torch!

------------------- -------------------

------------------- -------------------

------------------- -------------------

Pitch your tent here.

HOOWWL!

I don't want anyone to know my

SECRET MENACING SECRETS.

Write yours here and **keep them safe**
from **nosy** Softies.

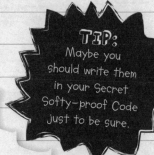

TIP:
Maybe you
should write them
in your Secret
Softy-proof Code
just to be sure.

YOUR TOP-SECRET SECRETS

SHHHHHHH!!!

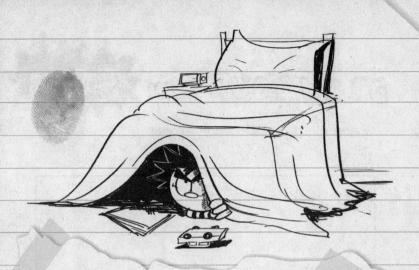

YOUR SECRET
HIDING PLACES

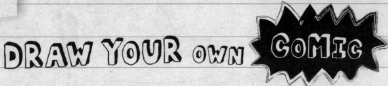

DRAW YOUR OWN COMIC

where aliens invade your street. . .

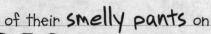

SCARE everyone out of their smelly pants on HALLOWEEN!

Draw your best, **most terrifying** costume here.

If you were a
50-FOOT-TALL MENAGE,
what would you look like? Draw yourself here.

What would you do?

Don't forget to draw that too!

RED and BLACK

These are my two most **favourite** colours.

Fill this <u>**entire page**</u> with <u>red-and-black</u> stripes.

It's time for the
MENACING GAMES!

A hole for Softies
to fall in!

Create
some events!

I've come up with a couple of

my own to get you started . . .

TIP: Make sure you can win every event!

MENACING EVENTS

◦ **Six-legged Race** (so Gnasher can join in)

- -

• **The High Pump** (see how high you can jump using only the power of **bottom-burps!**)

- -

•

- -

•

- -

•

- -

•

- -

•

- -

Draw a **MAP** of your
park or town,
and include all your favourite places
to hang out with your Menacing Mates.
Here's one of **BEANOTOWN!** ⟶

Draw your
map here!

Keep those UNWANTED SOFTY INTRUDERS from your door by using these pages to **design** your own super-menacing door plaques. (Just like my one!).

DENNIS'S BEDROOM NO SOFTIES EVER!

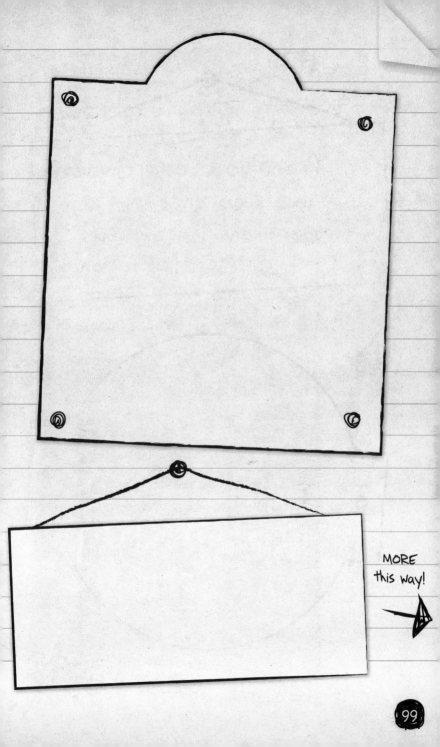

MORE
this way!

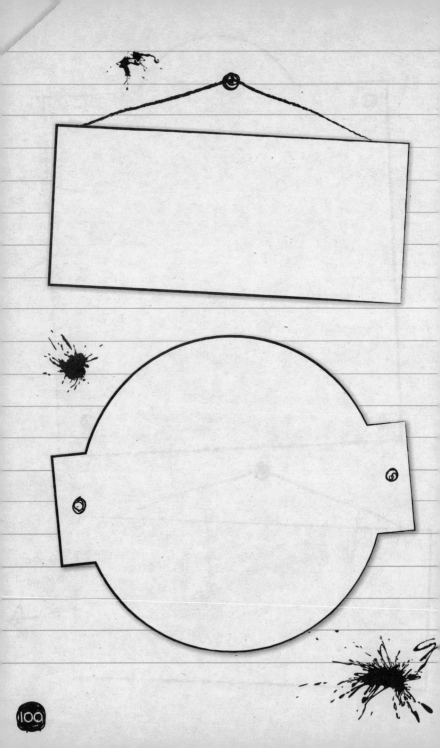

What am I **SHOUTING** about?

FOOD FIGHT with the
wet-lettuce Softies!

Complete this scene by drawing in all the grub
the Menaces are chucking at the Softies.

3, 2, 1 ... Let 'em have it!

Fed up with a sappy Softy? Design a

ROCKET JETPACK

to send them up into **space** and get them outta here!

It'll be better for all Menace-Kind!

Draw yourself on this **WANTED** poster, just like they used to in the Wild West. **Pew! Pew!** Don't forget to **write** at the bottom which **menacing acts** you're wanted for.

WANTED!

Draw yourself as a
SUPERHERO MENACE

and write a list
of all your
Super-Menace
super-duper
powers!

MY SUPER-MENACE POWERS

KERSPLATT!

KAPOW!!!

BOOM!!!

Answer this

MENACING QUESTIONNAIRE

to find out how <u>MEGA</u> a Menace you are.

1 You're up in your <u>tree house</u> and you see a Softy approaching down below. <u>What do you do?</u>

(A) **yank** in the ladder so they can't climb up

B Throw a bucket of stinky stuff on their head, then point and laugh

(C) **All of the above!**

2

You haven't done your <u>boring</u> spelling homework. Who do you **blame**?

A Your dog, for chewing it

B Your **little sister**, for being **sick** on it

C All of the above!

3

You have a **catapult** and some **mud**. <u>What</u> happens next?

A You load it up and use a **tree** for target practice

B You load it up and **fling** mud at every **Softy** you see

C All of the above!

4 It's dinner time! **What do you choose?**

A A giant Slopper-Gnosher-Gut-Bustin' Burger with Super-Loop Chips and **EXTRA** tomato sauce

B An **enormous** tub of Double Fatties' double-fat **ice cream**

DOUBLE FATTIES' DOUBLE FAT ICE CREAM

C All of the above!

5 You've heard there's a Softy convention coming to town. **What's your plan?**

A Plaster your town with <u>menacing posters</u> to scare the Softies away

B **Run!** Run like the wind! And don't come back for a year to be sure your town's **Softy-free**

C All of the above!

YOUR RESULTS

If you answered mostly Ⓐ...

You like the idea of being a Menace, but you still have a lot to learn. Keep reading my tips, Trainee Menace!

If you answered mostly B̲...

You are well on your way to becoming a Menace, but some further training is needed.

If you answered mostly G...

You are a MEGA-Menace. FULL STOP!

DRAW YOUR OWN COMIC

where you get a MASSIVE

prize for being a Mega-Menace . . .

TIP: Why not use some of these?

RRIPP!

BURST!

PLONK!

BUILD A MEGA-MENACING ROBOT

to help you take down the Softies!

SEED-ZAPPING EYE LASERS

PLANT-KILLER SPRAY GUN

ARRGH!

GARDEN-SHEAR HANDS

FLOWER-BED-STOMPING FEET

GNASHER LOVES SAUSAGES

GNNASSH!

Dream up the **weirdest,**
wackiest,
tastiest
sausage flavours you can, and write
them above the plates on the next page.

Then **draw** your sausages
on the plates!

TIP:
You might want to create some horrible flavours, too, as decoys for any Softies that come snooping!

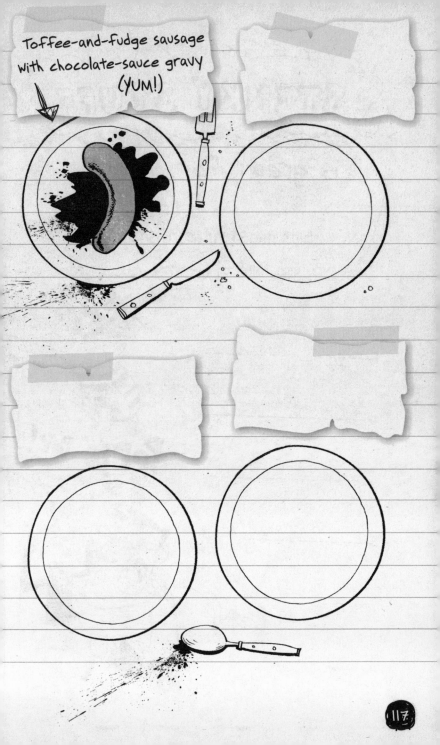

STINKY STUFF

is great for pranks.

List the **stinkiest stuff**
you can think of here.

_____

_____

_____

_____

_____

POP! POP!

What are you going to do with all that **stinky stuff?** Write your **pongiest** plans here.

TIP:
Stink bombs
are the best!

SKATEBOARDS
ROCK!

Plus they're the perfect getaway vehicle!

Design a super-cool skateboard here, and remember to include a menacing skateboard slogan!

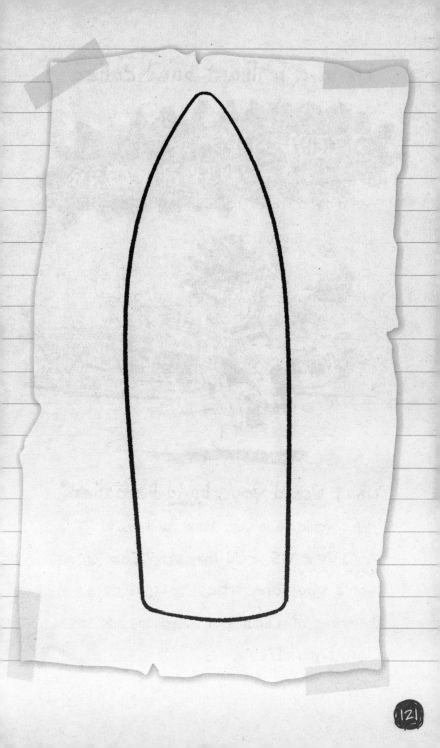

I'm in a brilliant band called

DENNIS AND THE DINMAKERS.

What would your <u>band</u> be called?

Who would be in your band, and what

instruments would they play? Come up with

some silly song titles too! (I've thrown in

the names of a couple of Dinmakers hits to

start you off.)

TIP:
Your songs can be whatever you like, as long as
you play them super-duper LOUD!!!

My band's name:

_____

Band members:

_____

_____

Our songs:

- Pants Disaster
- Chimp in My School
-
-
-

Draw a **cover** for your <u>band's album</u> here.

Now draw a **POSTER** for your own **FILM!**

Which **actor** would play you?

Make sure they are **mega** famous!!!

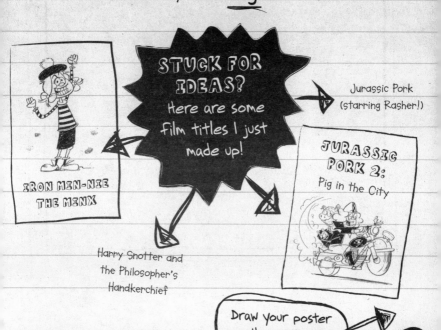

STUCK FOR IDEAS?
Here are some film titles I just made up!

IRON MIN-NIE THE MINX

Jurassic Pork (starring Rasher!)

JURASSIC PORK 2: Pig in the City

Harry Snotter and the Philosopher's Handkerchief

Draw your poster on the next page.

Write the <u>story</u> of your <u>film</u> here so that it's ready to be sent to **Hollywood.**

Turn **Walter-Wimp-Sniffle's**
DISGUSTING Softy flower into a
pranktastic **TRICK FLOWER!**

I hate flowers - they smell **horrid** and they attract Softies! Make all of these flowers **menacing** to **SCARE** the Softies away. Maybe you could turn one of them into a **Venus Softy-trap!**

BLOOM-TASTIC!

PARENTS

CAN BE SOOOOO BORING!

Write **lists** of **<u>funny pranks</u>** to play on them here.

Things to do to your DAD:

Set his alarm for 4.30 a.m. on Saturday morning. HA!

....

....

....

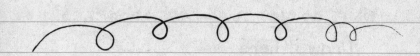

Things to do to your MUM:

Hide your **underpants** in the book she's reading as a stinky surprise!!!

What do you think just happened?
Draw it here.

I LOVE IT WHEN IT SNOWS

and you don't have to go to **school!**
No spelling tests, no homework . . .
BRILLIANT!

Instead I can do useful things like **building snowmen**. Or, better still,

snow-monsters!

Build your own **snow-monster** here.

SNOWBALL FIGHT!

Snow-one likes a <u>Softy</u>.

Draw yourself letting those

goody-goodies have it!

DRAW YOUR OWN COMIC

where you get turned into a dog . . .

URRGG!

CHOKE! CHOMP!

THIS IS MY
BEANOTOWN FLAG

Design a flag here for your town.

Once you've come up with a good one, make a
MASSIVE version, tape it to an
extra-long stick and wave it around!

MASKED MENACE!

Design a **mask** to **disguise** yourself

for all your **secret menacing missions**.

SCHOOL CAN BE SOOOOO BORING!

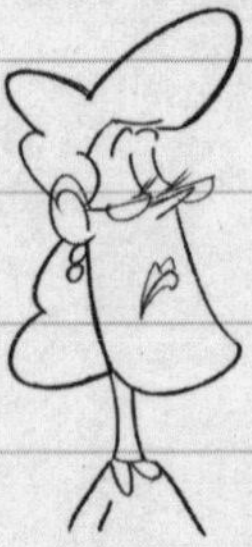

D.I.N.G. D.O.N.G.

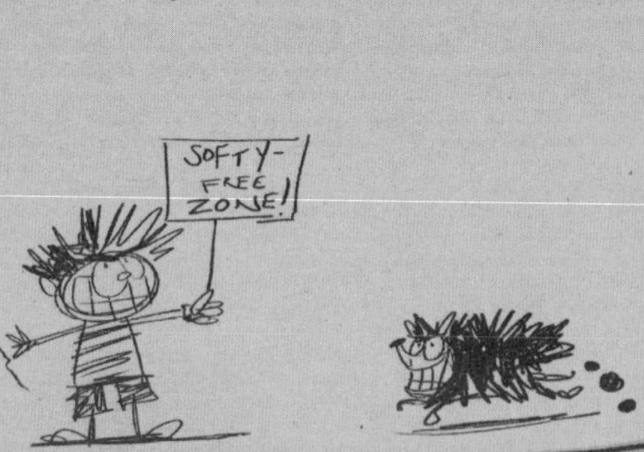

MATHS WORKBOOK

KEEP MENACING!

CREEPY-CRAWLIES

Sneaky critters have lots of **menacing potential!** Make a **note of any insects** you find while out and about, then use them as inspiration for your very own **super-silly menacing bug.** It'll be ideal for **scaring** Softies, and if it happens to crawl down the backs of their shirts then even better!

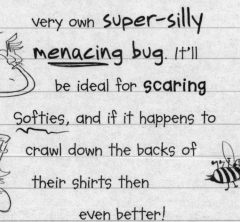

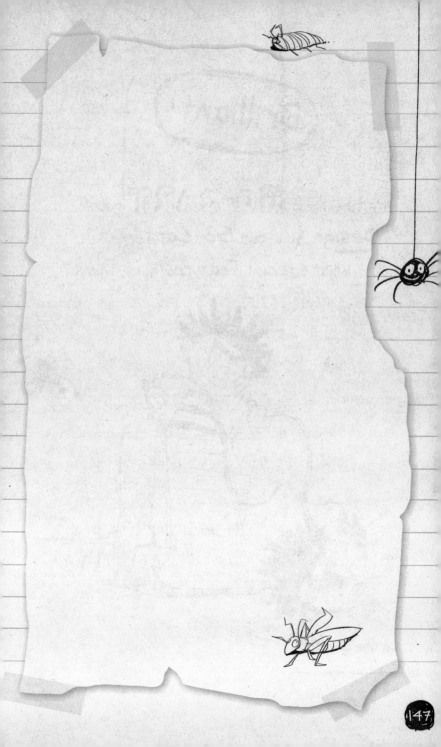

It's time for a **GO-CART** race!
<u>Des</u>ign your own Go-Cart.

What **special features** does it have?

MY MENACE-TASTIC
GO-CART!

Write your best MENACING JOKES

here, then try to say at least one every day!

HA!

Q: What do you call an alligator in a vest?
A: An investigator!

POP!

Q: What do get if you eat beans and onions?
A: Tear gas!

Q: Why did the burglar take a bath?
A: Because he wanted to make a clean getaway!

You've still got
LOADS
(of)
**MENACING
TO DO!**

Write a list of all the super—

menacing stuff you want to do

this year, then check back at

the end of the year to see if you

managed to do it all.

YOUR
MENACING
TO-DO LIST

....

....

....

....

....

....

....

CONGRATULATIONS!

You Menaced It Yourself!

Here's your trophy. Now fill in your name, **Menace Master!**

Welcome to the world of menacing!

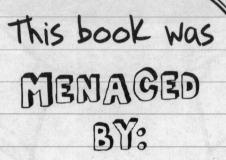